LIONS AND
LOBSTERS
AND FOXES
AND FROGS

LIONS AND LOBSTERS AND FOXES AND FROGS

FABLES FROM AESOP BY
ENNIS REES

DRAWINGS BY
EDWARD GOREY

YOUNG SCOTT BOOKS

Published by Young Scott Books, a Division of
The Addison-Wesley Publishing Co., Inc., Reading, Mass. 01867.
Library of Congress Catalog Card No. 75-155912.
Standard Book Number 201-09246-8.
Printed in U.S.A.

THE FABLES

THE DONKEY THAT FELL IN THE RIVER

A donkey loaded with salt
Was going across a river,
When, though it wasn't her fault,
She slipped and fell in, all aquiver.
But soon the salt melted, and she
Went on with a much lighter load,
At which she was pleased as could be
As she ambled on down the road.

The next day when she came to the stream
She was loaded up high with sponges,
But now she had started to dream
Of taking one of those plunges
That lighten the loads of a donkey.
So acting worse than a monkey,
She gave about two little lunges
And then a big one of those plunges
And purposely fell in the river,
For which we will have to forgive her.

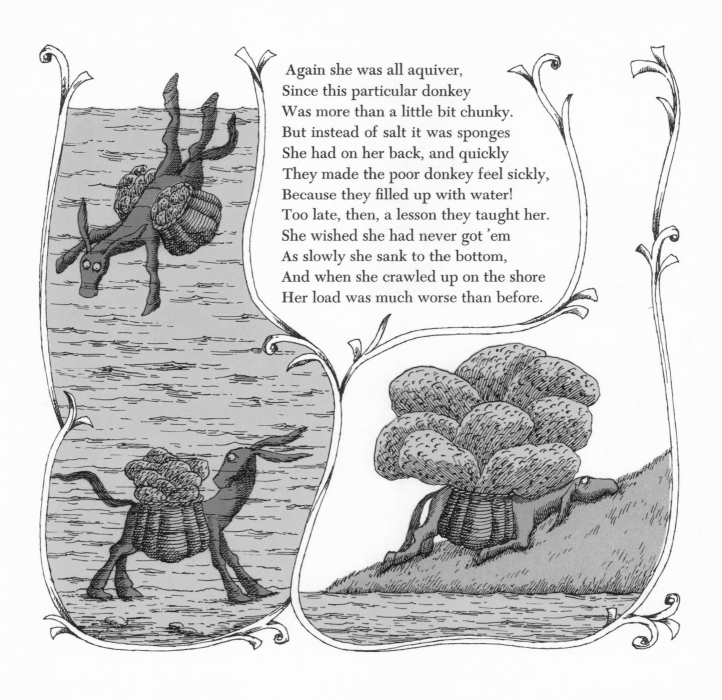

Again she was all aquiver,
Since this particular donkey
Was more than a little bit chunky.
But instead of salt it was sponges
She had on her back, and quickly
They made the poor donkey feel sickly,
Because they filled up with water!
Too late, then, a lesson they taught her.
She wished she had never got 'em
As slowly she sank to the bottom,
And when she crawled up on the shore
Her load was much worse than before.

THE WOLF

Mrs. Wolf did lots of bragging
   About all the children she had,
And sometimes it sounded like nagging
   And sometimes it wasn't so bad.

But one day a lioness came
   Who had just one little cub,
And Mrs. Wolf called by name
   All her children, to give them a rub.

Then she said to the lioness: "See
   How many nice children are mine.
Here are Willy, Milly, and Lee,
   All washed and fed and fine,

And this one I call Guy
   And this one's name is Brian."

THE DOG AND

A thirsty dog by the river Nile
Was so afraid that a crocodile
Would come up and catch him as he drank
That he wouldn't stop and drink from the bank
And so could do nothing better than
To run along and lap as he ran.
Then a crocodile, eager for slaughter,
Raised his head above the water
And called to the dog: "I say, what's the hurry?
I'd very much like to meet you, very!

THE CROCODILE

And I feel sure I would like you a lot.
So turn around and slow down to a trot
And come on back here to chat awhile,
And then, if you wish, you can run a mile."
"You honor me greatly," the dog shouted back.
"But you, I suspect, are in need of a snack,
And so indeed you'd like me—to chew!
But that would hardly make me like *you*.
In fact, the reason I drink as I flee
Is just to avoid your company."

THE FROG

A young rat out looking for something to do,
Especially something exciting and new,
Ran into a frog on the bank of a pond.
Said the frog, "You know I'm exceedingly fond
Of rats. Come down in the pond on a visit.
I'll show you some things that are really exquisite."

AND THE RAT

Now the heat that day was furious
And the rat very young and curious.
He thought a dip in the pond would be swell,
But warned the frog that he couldn't swim well.
"No matter at all," was the frog's reply.
"Just come here close and let me tie
Your ankle to mine with a piece of this grass,
And since I can swim as well as a bass,
I'll tow you along and help you swim."
Well this seemed an excellent plan to him,
So the rat came close and got himself tied
And in they plunged, side by side.

Very soon the rat had enough and more
And he begged the frog to take him to shore,
But the treacherous frog just looked all around,
Then pulled the rat under until he drowned.
And next he began to untie the grass
That held him to the dead rat, when alas,

Before he could get the grass untied,
Though frantically the cruel frog tried,
Along came a hawk, who could hardly help gloating
When he looked down and saw the rat floating.
So swooping he caught him up in his talons,
The rat *and* the frog, both dripping gallons,
For that hawk had caught both seafood and meat
And all because of the frog's deceit.

THE IMPATIENT FOX

One morning a fox who was eager to eat
Found in an old hollow oak some meat
That shepherds had left till time for dinner.
Now since the fox had no wish to get thinner,
He slipped through the rather narrow crack
And ate till he had emptied the sack
In which the shepherds had left their dinner.
And then he wished that he *could* get thinner,
Since now, as he quite quickly found,
His stomach was so very tight and round
That he was unable to set himself free.
He could not even squeeze through the crack
     in the tree.

All he could do was mutter and scowl
And whine and fuss and holler and howl.
At last another fox heard him yelp
And came to ask him how he could help.
"How?" said the fox who was trapped in the tree.
"Just think of something. Don't ask me."
"Well," said the other, "I wish I knew
Some way of quickly comforting you.
But it looks to me that you'll never get out
Anymore of yourself than maybe your snout
Until once again you are just as thin
As you were this morning when you got in."

THE SNAKE'S TAIL

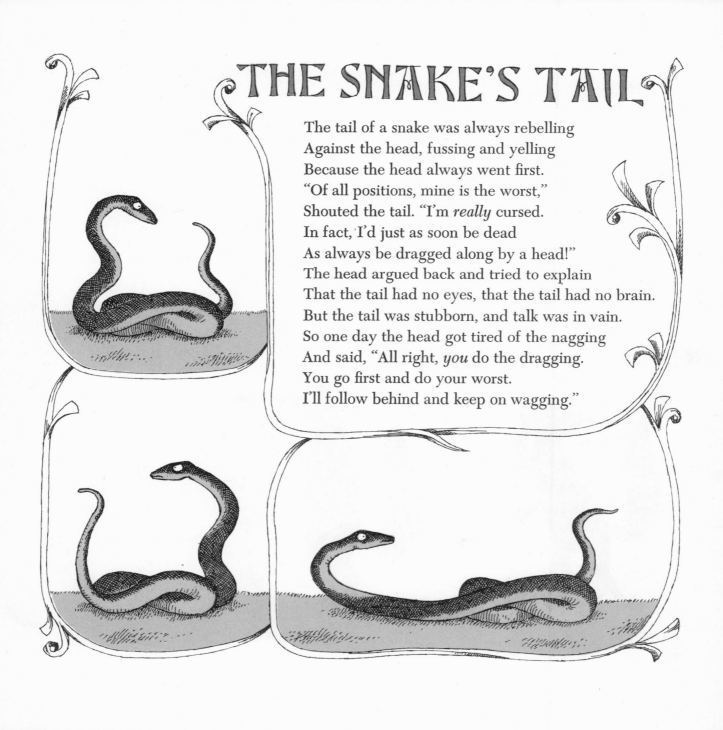

The tail of a snake was always rebelling
Against the head, fussing and yelling
Because the head always went first.
"Of all positions, mine is the worst,"
Shouted the tail. "I'm *really* cursed.
In fact, I'd just as soon be dead
As always be dragged along by a head!"
The head argued back and tried to explain
That the tail had no eyes, that the tail had no brain.
But the tail was stubborn, and talk was in vain.
So one day the head got tired of the nagging
And said, "All right, *you* do the dragging.
You go first and do your worst.
I'll follow behind and keep on wagging."

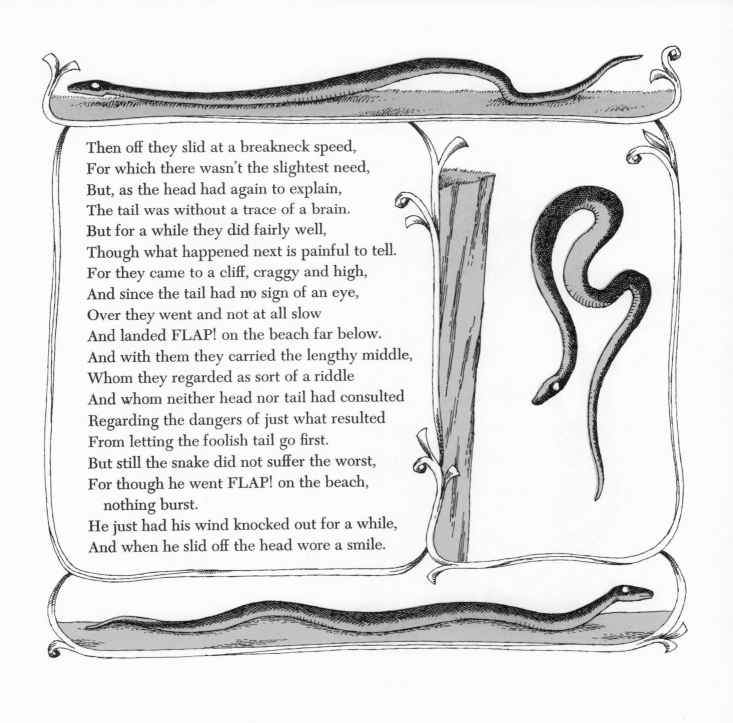

Then off they slid at a breakneck speed,
For which there wasn't the slightest need,
But, as the head had again to explain,
The tail was without a trace of a brain.
But for a while they did fairly well,
Though what happened next is painful to tell.
For they came to a cliff, craggy and high,
And since the tail had no sign of an eye,
Over they went and not at all slow
And landed FLAP! on the beach far below.
And with them they carried the lengthy middle,
Whom they regarded as sort of a riddle
And whom neither head nor tail had consulted
Regarding the dangers of just what resulted
From letting the foolish tail go first.
But still the snake did not suffer the worst,
For though he went FLAP! on the beach,
   nothing burst.
He just had his wind knocked out for a while,
And when he slid off the head wore a smile.

A partridge, perched in a low little tree,
Was approached by a fox, who said, "I agree,
Mrs. Partridge, with all the creatures I've heard
Say what a perfectly beautiful bird
They think you are. For it would be cruel
Not to admit that your beak is a jewel.
You're lovely, my dear, and sure to remain so,
Since all of your feathers are so like a rainbow.
But most creatures look more lovely, it's true,
When they are asleep, and so would you."

THE PARTRIDGE

So Mrs. Partridge, with one coy peep,
Closed her eyes for a beauty sleep,
Which didn't last long at all, because
She at once found herself in the fox's jaws.
"My gracious!" said she. "How you can bound!
You must be the finest leaper around.
Why I had no idea, I just didn't know,
That you could jump up and catch me so.
But what outdoes your leaping, I claim,
Is the sound of your voice when you say my name.
Oh, won't you say it once more at least?
Then go ahead and enjoy your feast."

At this the fox opened his mouth with a grin,
Whereat Mrs. Partridge flippered his chin
And flew up to perch on a tree's very peak.
"Now why in the world did I want to speak?"
Said the fox. "Because," chirped the bird in reply,
"You're almost as easy to flatter as I."

THE ANT AND THE GRASSHOPPER

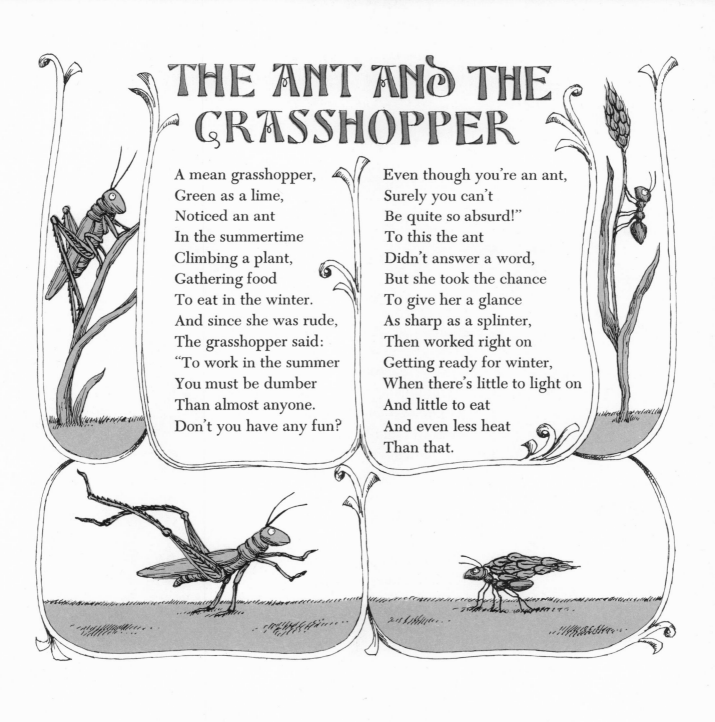

A mean grasshopper,
Green as a lime,
Noticed an ant
In the summertime
Climbing a plant,
Gathering food
To eat in the winter.
And since she was rude,
The grasshopper said:
"To work in the summer
You must be dumber
Than almost anyone.
Don't you have any fun?

Even though you're an ant,
Surely you can't
Be quite so absurd!"
To this the ant
Didn't answer a word,
But she took the chance
To give her a glance
As sharp as a splinter,
Then worked right on
Getting ready for winter,
When there's little to light on
And little to eat
And even less heat
Than that.

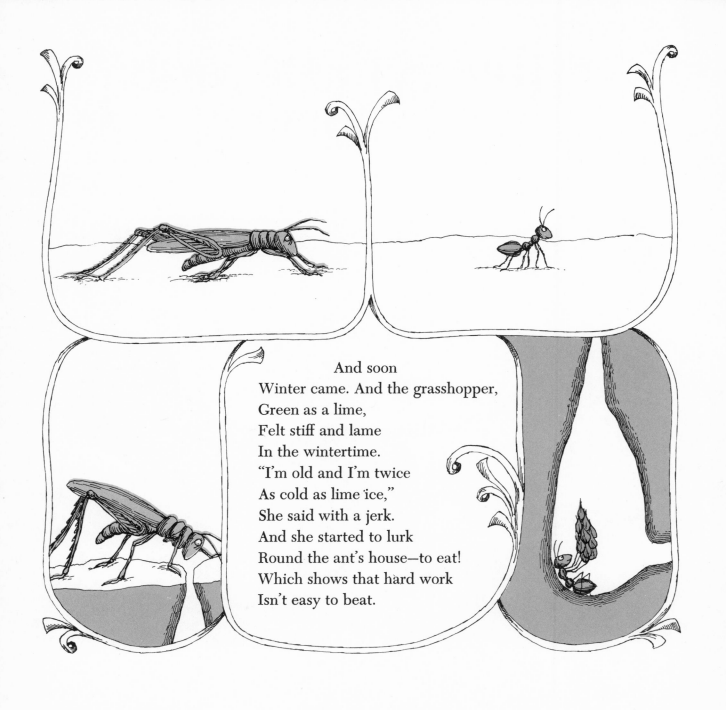

And soon
Winter came. And the grasshopper,
Green as a lime,
Felt stiff and lame
In the wintertime.
"I'm old and I'm twice
As cold as lime ice,"
She said with a jerk.
And she started to lurk
Round the ant's house—to eat!
Which shows that hard work
Isn't easy to beat.

THE DOG AND THE LION

A dog one day
Was loudly pursuing
A powerful lion,
And this he was doing
With all of the speed
He could put in each bound,
When all of a sudden
The lion turned round!

And the dog stopped short
Almost in mid-air,
Reversed his course
And almost his hair,
And ran even faster
From his prey
Than he had been running
The other way.

THE CONCEITED FROG

An ox eating grass in a bog
Stepped on a very small frog.
Now the big ox had no wish
To make the small frog go squish,
And he went where the grass was less bad
Without even knowing he had.

When Mother Frog came from the pond,
She did her best to respond
As first one child, then another
Told her what happened to Brother.
They said that something gigantic
Had driven all of them frantic
And made poor Brother go squoosh!
To this, Mother Frog said, "Shoosh!"
And swelling up with a hiss,
She inquired, "Was the thing big as this?"

"Oh bigger, Mother, much bigger,"
The little frogs cried with a snigger.
So she kept swelling and swelling
And they kept yelling and yelling,
For she thought Mother Frog
Was the biggest thing in the bog,
Or certainly should be, at least,
And soon she became quite a beast.

She became with hot air so loaded
That finally she exploded.

THE LION AND THE MOUSE

A mouse ran over the nose
    Of a sleeping lion,
Whereat the lion arose—
    A *leaping* lion!

He seized the mouse in his paw
    And was going to eat him,
But stopped when he looked down and saw
    That the mouse would entreat him.

"Spare me!" cried the mouse, "and someday
    I'll do you a favor.
You I will surely repay.
    Someday I'll be braver."

The lion laughed and released him,
    A poor little beast,
But soon the same mouse greatly pleased him,
    To say the poor least.

For the lion got caught in a net
    By a hunter, his foe,
And the mouse gnawed the cord and let
    The good lion go.

THE MOTHER LOBSTER AND HER DAUGHTER

A boiled lobster's shell of bright red
Was found by a young lady lobster who said:
"Oh Mother, just look·at the beautiful shell
Of some lady lobster we didn't know well.
In fact, I never before have seen
Any lobster at all who wasn't green,
Or a kind of greenish grayish brown..
This must have been a lobster from town,
And now I'll never be satisfied
Until I can go and get myself dyed
Like that lobster did, somewhere in town."

"Vain creature," her mother said with a frown,
"Just as sure as you are my daughter
That lobster died in boiling water,
And if you don't want to wind up in a pot
You'd better stop wishing to be what you're not!"

THE BAT AND THE CATS

A fat cat sat
On the wing of a bat
And teased the poor beast
Before having a feast.
The bat begged for her life,
But the fat cat's wife
Said, "Don't be absurd.
We can't spare a bird."
"But," said the bat,
"I'm not a bird.
Don't *you* be absurd!
I'd as soon be a gnat
As a bird. Can't you see?
Just as sure as can be
I'm a poor little mouse
On my way to the house."

So the fat cat bowed
And politely allowed
The bat to go free.

But it wasn't three
Whole days after that
When the very same bat
Was caught by another,
The fat cat's brother.
Of mice he caught many,
But this cat was skinny.
And there the cat sat
On the wing of the bat
And teased the poor beast
Before having a feast.
The bat begged for her life,
But the skinny cat's wife
Said, "Don't be a louse.
We can't spare a mouse."
"But," said the bat,
"I'm not a mouse.
Don't *you* be a louse!
I'd as soon be a gnat
As a mouse. Can't you see?
Just as sure as can be
I'm a poor little bird
Who wants to be heard."

So the skinny cat bowed
And politely allowed
The bat to go free.
Sometimes, you see,
It comes in quite handy,
And can be just dandy,
To be like the bat
Who could fool any cat
And to have, as did she,
Something else you can be.

THE FLIES AND THE HONEY

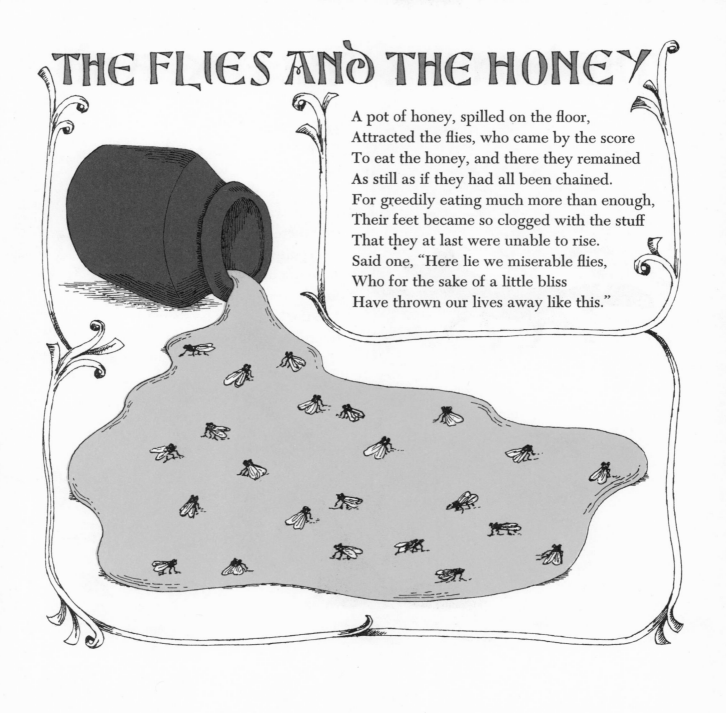

A pot of honey, spilled on the floor,
Attracted the flies, who came by the score
To eat the honey, and there they remained
As still as if they had all been chained.
For greedily eating much more than enough,
Their feet became so clogged with the stuff
That they at last were unable to rise.
Said one, "Here lie we miserable flies,
Who for the sake of a little bliss
Have thrown our lives away like this."

THE DONKEY, THE FOX, AND

A fox and a donkey agreed
To help each other in need
By hunting at times together.
But then the fox wondered whether
To sacrifice the donkey,
For she wasn't feeling too spunky
And there in the midst of the wood
She spotted where a lion stood!
So to the lion she sped,
And he promised that if she led
The donkey where he should be brought
In order to be well caught,
He would let her off without harm.

THE LION

Then using all of her charm,
She led the donkey around
Till he fell in a hole in the ground.
But the lion no sooner saw
That the donkey was under his paw
Than he roared a few big haw-haw's
And seized the fox in his jaws!
So instead of letting her be,
He ate her first, you see.

THE THOROUGHBRED

A thoroughbred dog was having a talk
With a puppy of his while out for a walk,
When all of the village mongrels and mutts
Gathered around them and made them the butts
Of loudly barked out insults and slurs.
"Dad," said the pup, "let's finish the curs."

AND THE MONGRELS

"Patience, my child," his father said.
"If all the mongrels and mutts were dead,
How would you know a thoroughbred?"

THE FROGS WHO

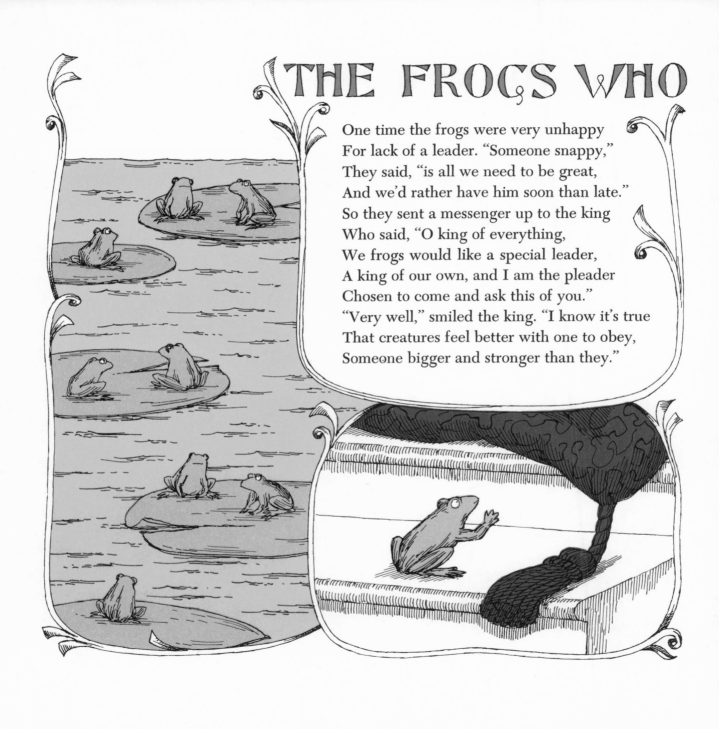

One time the frogs were very unhappy
For lack of a leader. "Someone snappy,"
They said, "is all we need to be great,
And we'd rather have him soon than late."
So they sent a messenger up to the king
Who said, "O king of everything,
We frogs would like a special leader,
A king of our own, and I am the pleader
Chosen to come and ask this of you."
"Very well," smiled the king. "I know it's true
That creatures feel better with one to obey,
Someone bigger and stronger than they."

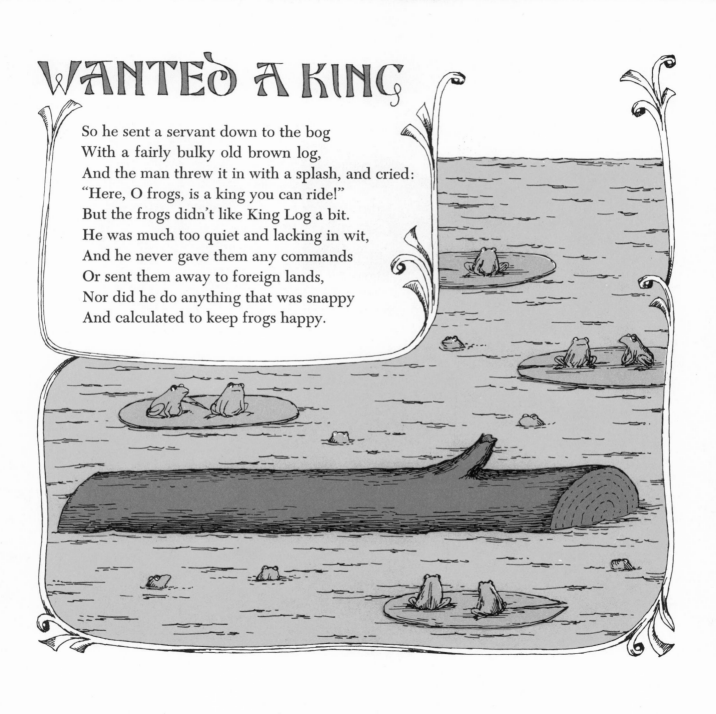

WANTED A KING

So he sent a servant down to the bog
With a fairly bulky old brown log,
And the man threw it in with a splash, and cried:
"Here, O frogs, is a king you can ride!"
But the frogs didn't like King Log a bit.
He was much too quiet and lacking in wit,
And he never gave them any commands
Or sent them away to foreign lands,
Nor did he do anything that was snappy
And calculated to keep frogs happy.

So they complained to the high king again,
Who now lost his patience and sent them a crane,
Who proved very snappy indeed as their leader,
For since he was truly an endless eater,
Every time a poor frog followed him
He snapped him up and greedily swallowed him!